To Sophia
Christmas, 2012
from Grandma

HARRY TAYLOR
WHO DAT DOG?

written by

Alden Taylor

illustrated by

Winifred Barnum-Newman

Mascot Publishing
www.mascotbooks.com

Text Copyright © 2011 Alden Taylor

Illustration Copyright © 2011 Winifred Barnum-Newman

All rights reserved. Published 2011

Library of Congress Cataloguing-in-Publication Data

Taylor, Alden • Harry Taylor - Who Dat Dog?

Barnum-Newman, Winifred, illustrator.

ISBN - 13:978-1-937406-07-03
ISBN - 10:1-937406-07-5

(Fiction - Children - New Orleans) Title

Printed in the United States of America

Book/cover design by Winifred Barnum-Newman
Back cover photograph by 'Leo & Jenny Photography'

Mascot Books
www.mascotbooks.com

To Harry Taylor - my muse

To Grandpa and Toby - for always being there

To Ian and Mary - for choosing New Orleans

To Graham, Jamie and Millie for their input and support

To Susie - for her faith in the Who Dat Nation

To Bettie Jackson - for all the good times

and, especially,

To the many unsung heroes of New Orleans and

Lousiana who are working so hard

to rebuild their city and state

From the Author

I love New Orleans! My dog, Harry, and I have spent a lot of time there visiting my son, his wife, and their dog, Louie, whom they adopted after Hurricane Katrina.

I am continually impressed by the people I've met in Lousiana. Their courage, dignity and resilience in the face of so much tragedy should be an inspiration to all of us.

I wanted to write a book honoring the spirit of New Orleans. To me, it was truly on display after the New Orleans Saints won the 2010 Super Bowl. The whole city came together in a memorable celebration of recovery and hope. Harry and I had a great time rejoicing with the Who Dat Nation.

In his everyday life Harry Taylor is a certified Reading Therapy dog, and he loves listening to children read dog-themed books to him. He hopes you will enjoy reading this book to your dog, cat, parakeet, family or friends!

HARRY TAYLOR

WHO DAT DOG?

Who Dat Dog walking
down the street?

It's Harry Taylor,
a nose with four feet.

That nose is Harry's
most important part,

along with his paws,
tail and heart.

Harry is a Hound with the
best sense of smell.

He can find a cat
in an old church bell,

or a hamburger hidden
on a red tugboat,

even a parakeet
under a float.

In New Orleans
Mardi Gras's here

With lots of parades
and loads of cheer!

The Saints just won
the Super Bowl.

The Crescent City
is on a roll.

Everyone's dancing and
covered with beads,

dogs are running
without any leads.

Who Dat Dog Harry
is one of those

who's roaming the streets
and tapping his toes.

A call goes out
for the Barkus Parade,

a special, DOGS ONLY,
masquerade.

The Lead Dog is Simon,
a dog with black spots,

who's dressed as a chef,
and carrying pots.

But help! Good Heavens!
Where is his hat?

He certainly can't lead
the parade without that!

"Where dat dog Harry?",
the people cry,

"We need your help!"
Fly! Fly! Fly!

Harry sniffs Simon
and off he goes,

howling out loud
as he follows his nose.

Down to the docks
and all the tugboats,

to the French Quarter
and Mardi Gras floats.

Around Jackson Square
with a stop at a church,

a snack at Aunt Sally's
and resuming his search,

he hops on the street car
with a Who Dat Dog bark,

and travels out
to Audubon Park.

15

His nose leads him directly
to the park Zoo.

The crowds part
as he barks his way through,

to the African Savanna,
lions and gazelles,

and the main attraction,
a giraffe named Nells.

Harry is so little,
and Nells so tall,

that he has to climb up

onto a wall.

He stretches his neck

and tries to see

what his nose has led him to,
up in a tree.

Hooray! There it is!
Simon's chef hat,

perched on a branch,
and in it, there sat,

four baby birds,
fluffy and sweet,

waiting for Mama
to bring them a treat.

Who Dat Dog Harry,
he howls full blast

'til Simon and Pete
find him at last.

Pete arrives in his truck
and with careful hands

takes the nest over
to where Harry stands.

Now what to do?
They need a new home.

They're just baby birds,
and too young to roam.

Bettie, the zoo-keeper,
saves the day with a

New Orleans Saints helmet!
Hip, hip, hooray!

Harry checks twice,
just to be sure

the birds are now happy,
safe and secure.

Goodbye to the babies,
Bettie, and Nells.

"We love you, Harry!"
the zoo crowd yells.

Harry drives back
with Simon and Pete.

The Who Dat Dog
is feeling upbeat.

And guess who leads
the Barkus Parade?

Simon, the Chef and
Harry, his aide.

GLOSSARY

Audubon Park - a 400-acre park on New Orleans' western edge. It houses a 100-year old golf-course, a park and a zoo.

Aunt Sally's - a store that was started in the 1930's, selling pralines. Pralines are a French candy made of Louisiana pecans, stirred in boiling sugar until crisp and brown.

Barkus Parade - dogs get dressed up for this parade (a spoof on the famous Bacchus Parade) where "cats are welcome but security is not provided".

Crescent City - the original settlement was tucked in the crescent-shaped bend in the Missis-sippi River.

Fleur-de-Lis - "Flower of the Lily". The official symbol for the state of Louisiana, and a sign of hope since Hurricane Katrina.

GLOSSARY (con't)

Jackson Square - "The Heart of New Orleans" was originally called Place d'Armes, where the signing of the Louisiana Purchase was celebrated. After the Battle of New Orleans, it was renamed Jackson Square in honor of the victor, Andrew Jackson.

Mardi Gras (or Carnival) - a prolonged party that begins on January 6 (Three Kings Day) and continues until Mardi Gras Day (Fat Tuesday), the day before Lent. New Orleans celebrates with about 80 parades citywide.

New Orleans Saints - NFL team that won the 2010 Super Bowl, beating the Indianapolis Colts, 31-17.

"Who dat" - a local expression originating from asking "Who's that?" when someone is at the door.

A GAME FOR YOU!

Find the items listed below!
How many of each one can you find?
Write the number in the square next to each item.

bandana ☐

beads ☐

cat ☐

confetti ☐

fleur-de-lis ☐

hamburger ☐

parakeet ☐

baby birds ☐

spoon ☐